Super Scribbles

Superheroes

Parragon

Superheroes

Doodle your way through this super book.
Don't forget ... you can use your stickers,
stencils, and patterned paper
anywhere you like.

Draw, stick, and stencil on each page to
create the most incredible superheroes,
weird aliens, crooked pirates, scary monsters
and dinosaurs, and cool robots!

ZAP! POW!

Can you turn this normal schoolboy and girl into superheroes?
Doodle some more mini heroes of your own.

This pair are ready to fight crime together.
Design an outfit for the superhero's sidekick.

ZPP! This superhero has found the secret headquarters of a super villain! What can he see with his amazing X-ray vision?

Create a superhero to rescue this girl.
Give your superhero a cool cape.

Who would wear these superhero masks?
Design three superhero costumes to match these sneaky diguises.

Invent your very own super team by designing some hero heads and bodies.
What super powers do they each have?

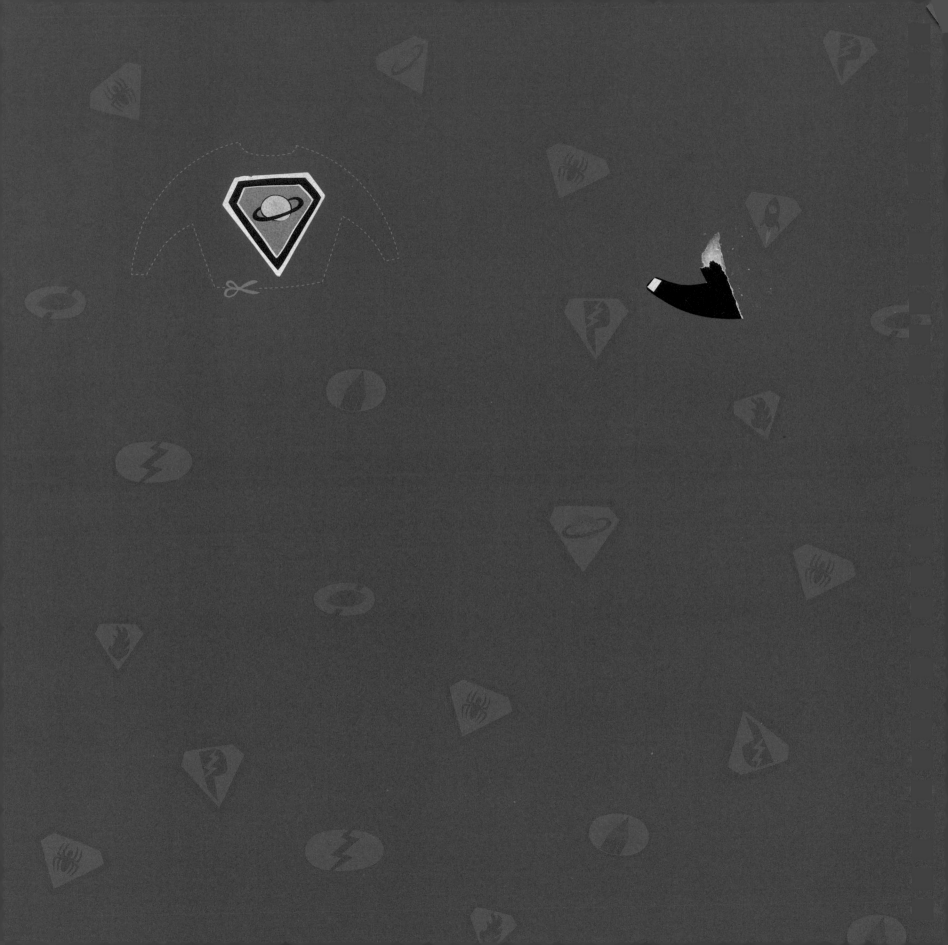

Aliens

Aliens

Design an alien!
Invent an intergalactic alien friend here.

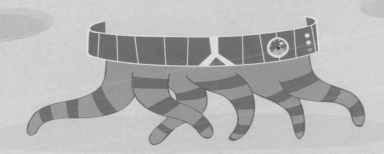

Finish drawing this **TALL** alien and create a friend for him.
Use your stickers to give the aliens as many eyes as you like.

JET

Mor.sseled

Give this planet a name, then doodle a family of aliens to live on it.

blip, blip, blip!

Who's taking off on a space adventure in this alien ship?
Add some alien passengers and more stars, moons, and planets to outer space.

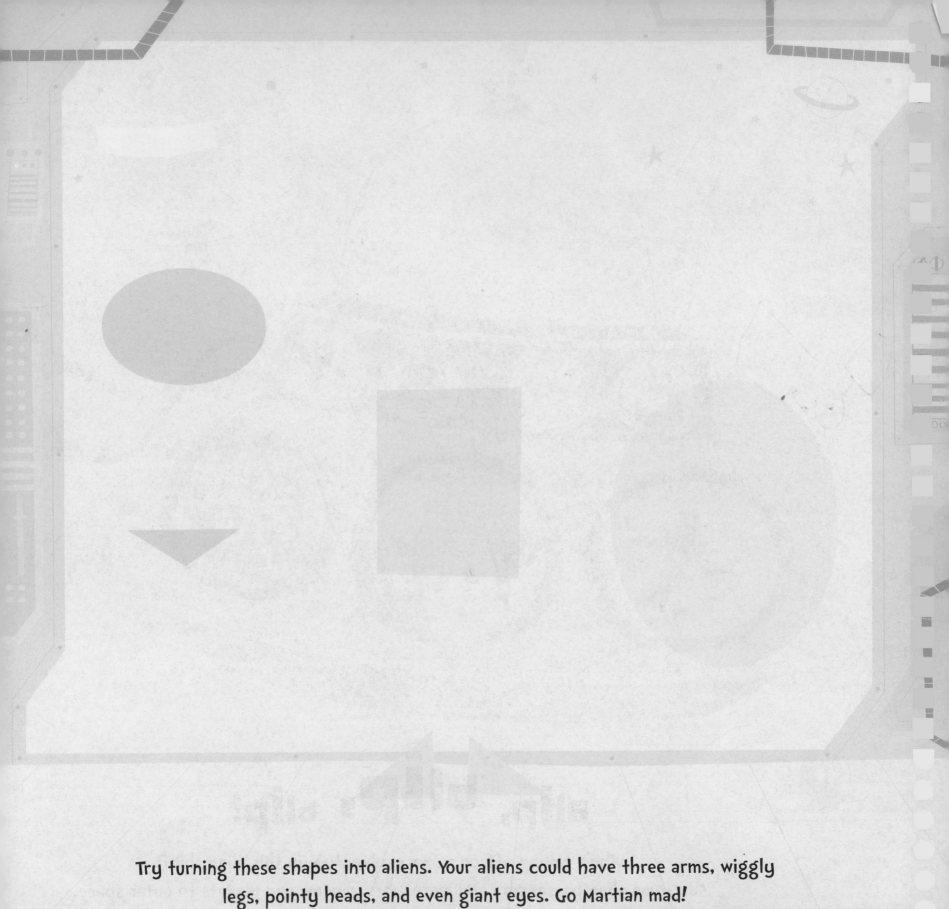

Try turning these shapes into aliens. Your aliens could have three arms, wiggly
legs, pointy heads, and even giant eyes. Go Martian mad!

This flying saucer needs an alien captain to land it on the planet.
Use your stencils and stickers to add patterns to the spaceship.

ed alert!

raw or stick on more spotted blue aliens if you want to help them defend the planet or add more green spaceships if the invaders are going to win!

Pirates

Pirates

Who is walking the plank?

Is it the captain or a trouble-making member of his crew?

AHOY there, Shipmates!

Turn these landlubbers into pirates by inventing some swashbuckling pirate outfits.

Who's a pretty boy then?
Draw a parrot on the captain's shoulder with
multicolored feathers.

Help this pirate galleon set sail by adding sails and decorating its deck.
Doodle your own pirate crew!

Aye-aye, Captain!

Use stickers, stencils, and patterned paper to fill in everything between the captain's hat and his wooden leg.

Add some loot to the pirates' chest.
Use your stickers to fill it up with gold coins and diamonds!

Land-ho! The pirates have spotted a treasure island.
Add some extra stickers to the map, so the pirates
are ready to go treasure hunting!

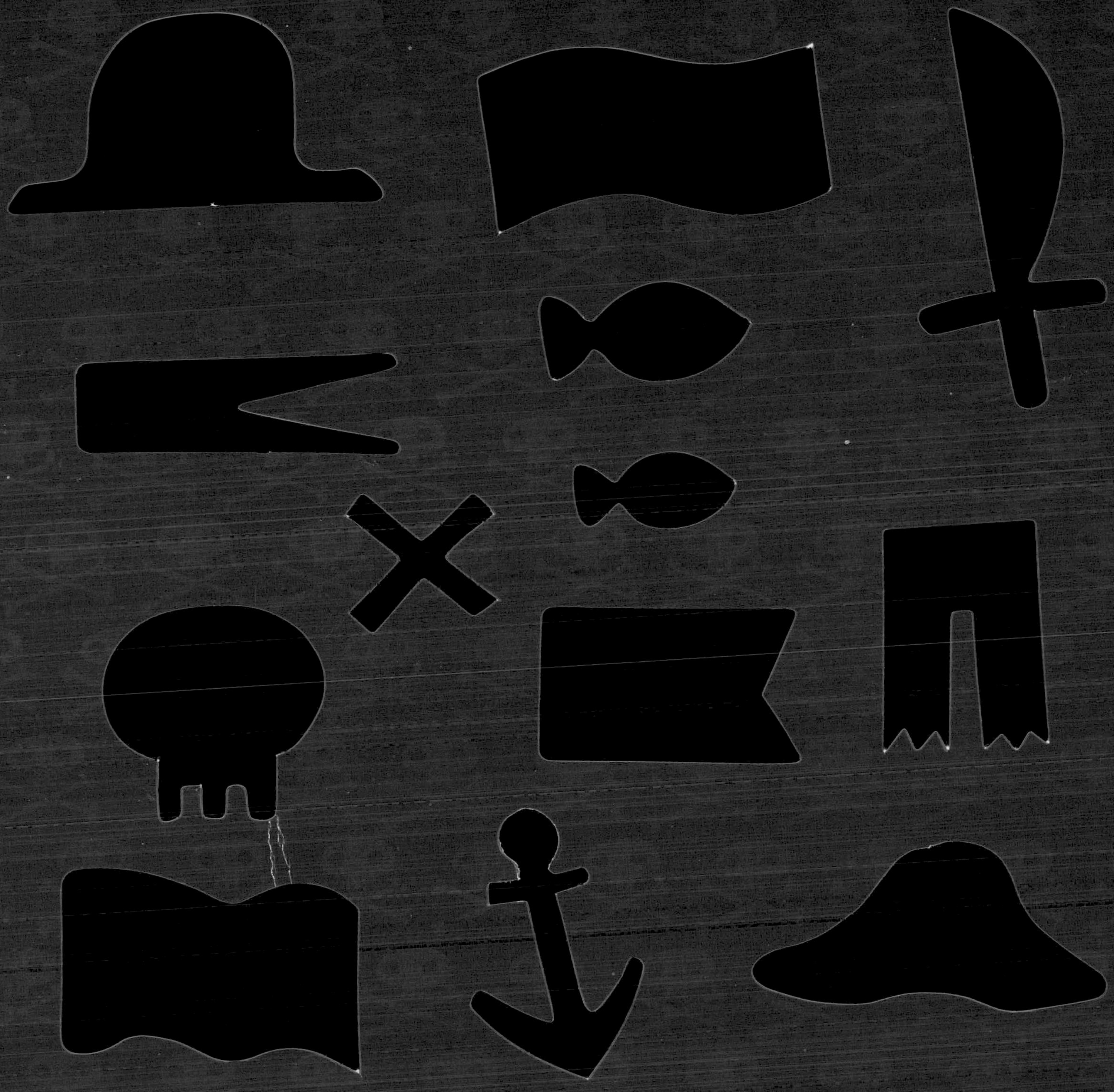

Monsters and Dinos

Monsters and Dinos

How many monsters or dinos can you draw here?

It's **monster** mayhem!
How many more monsters can you squeeze on the bus?

Some kinds of dinos have stripy plates and some have spotted skin!
Doodle prehistoric patterns on these dinos.

Grrrrr! Draw a monster head for each of these ugly monster mouths!

What do you think this dino eats?
Fill up his mouth and his plate with dino food.

WANTED!

GLEB

- -

for causing terrible trouble all over town.

Monster reward offered.
Signed the Mayor of Monsterville

Uh-oh! This monster is in BIG trouble.
Design a trouble-making monster and give him a cool name to finish the wanted poster.

Look out for this huge dinosaur!
Bring him to life with super colorful doodles.

KEEP OUT!

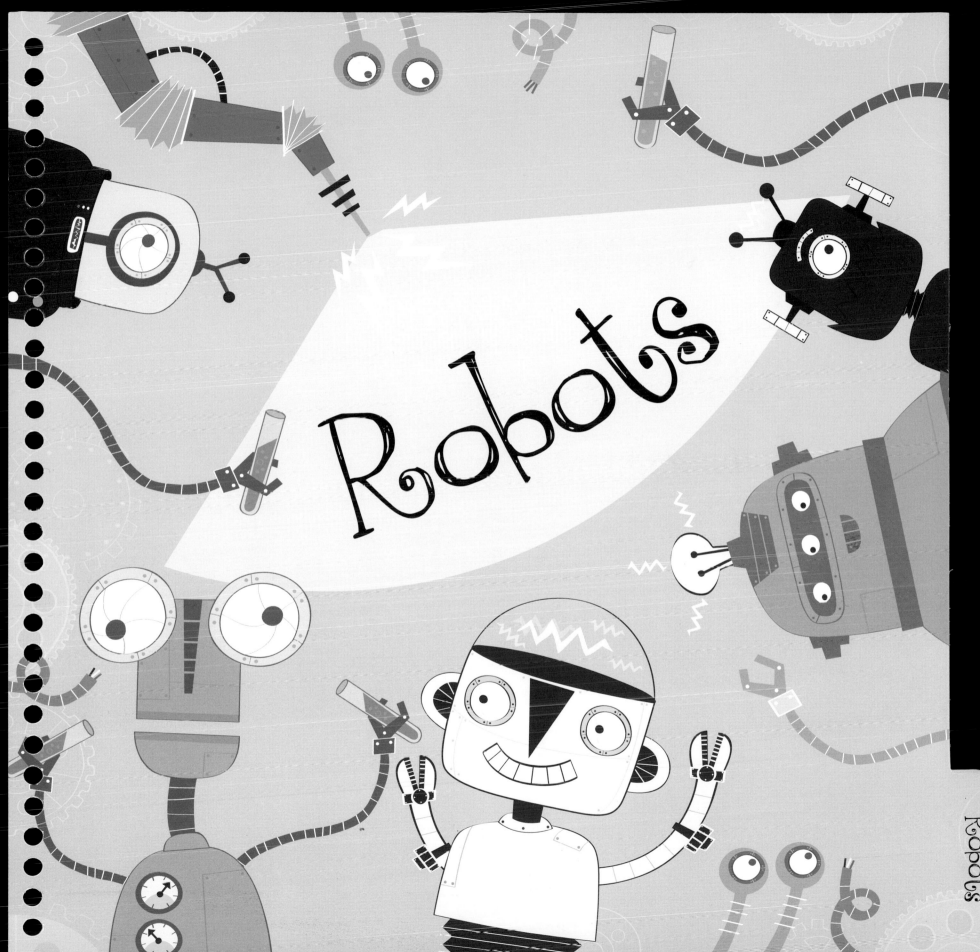

Robots

Robots

Use your stencils and stickers to design a doodle bot

What's the **mad** scientist building in his lab? Invent a brand new robot with your stickers!

Clunk, clank! Draw the other half of this robot.

What kind of robot casts a shadow like this?
Design a real robot to match the creepy shadow!

Creeeeeak! Add arms and legs to these robots.

THE DAILY GADGET

Over 3 in Long!

Snap Clackle and Jet

PROFESSOR A. BOFFIN INVENTS EXCELLENT NEW ROBOT

WOW!

Doodle the professor's new creation on this newspaper clipping, then give it a name.

How are these robots feeling?
Add a different face to each robot head.

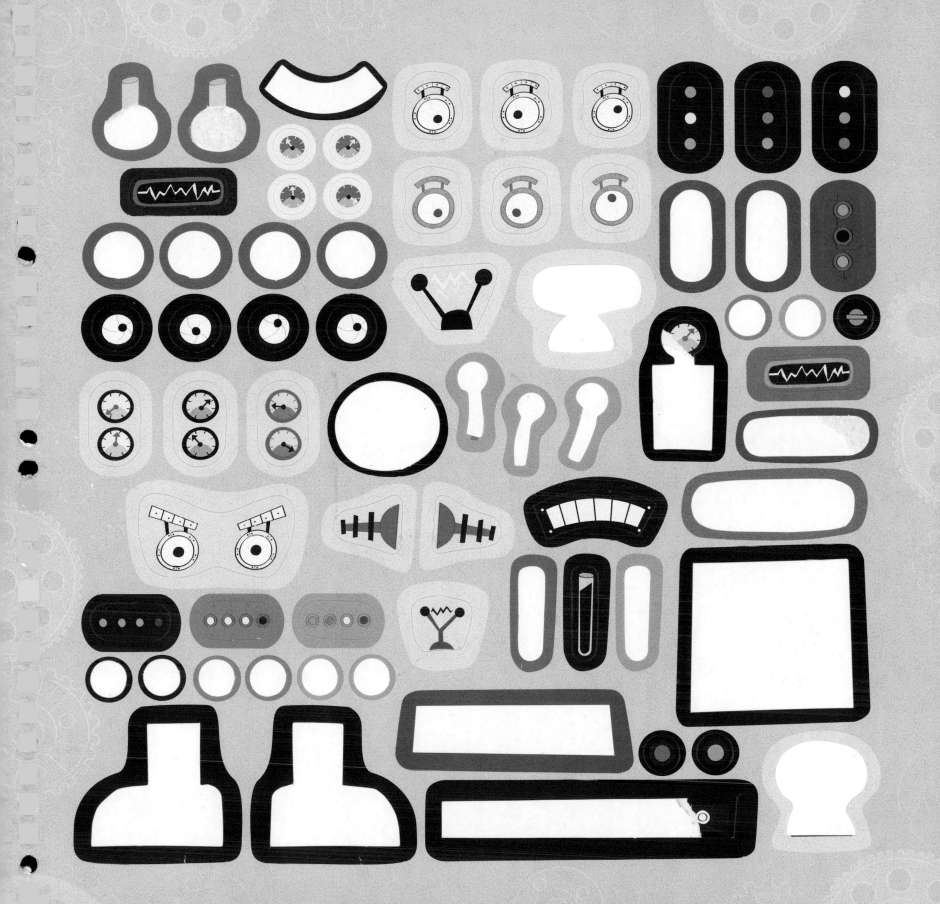